of

a

Butterflyy

Poetry Collection

L.N. MALLORY
AKA POECTICC SERENITYY

First Published 2020

ISBN 9781513665405

Printed in USA by Kindle

Cover Designed by J Ash B Designs

Editing by Sabrena Jones-Pole @sabrenasharonne

DEDICATION

First and foremost, to my Lord and Savior, Jesus Christ. Without my faith, I know I would not be where I am today. I thank God for the gift of writing. To be able to paint pictures with words.

I also dedicate this to my amazing family, my husband and children. To my entire family and friends.

And last but definitely not least, my daddy and mommy! I know that they are smiling down from heaven. I love you both.

CONTENTS

CHAPTER ONE

Tears of Love

REIGN

My king, my love,
Don't ever give up.
You have come too far
To turn back around
Continue to stand your ground
The enemy will try to tear you down.
But my prayers will keep you up,
Covering you
No weapon formed against you shall prosper
Burdens you don't have
To bear alone
I'm here too
Look at me,

Look into my eyes
See the pain I feel inside.
When I see you down
My love,
Put on your crown
Show the world your glory
Give them the great man,
No longer defeated
Now uplifted
Go
It's time to
Reign.

GOLDEN BEAUTY

How magnificent to see
Long lasting love
Forever matrimony
Time seemed like forever
But was only a wink in time
Uprooted like a fall leaf
Carried away by the autumn breeze
Colors changed in our lifetime also
Reflects the seasons of our journey
Final chapters of this lifespan
Together forever
You said as you held my hand
Only time to let go,
Is when God says so.

THE DOOR

If you can't love me
With passion
Then don't love me at
All
I don't want a cup half
Full,
I want it to overflow.
I want more,
Then I can hold.
If you can't do that,
There's the door.

THE BEHOLDER

Beauty is in the eye of the beholder
But who is beholding the eye?
You or I?
Who is right?
Who is wrong?
Who has greater sight?
I might not see what you see,
You might not see what I see.
In the end,
We all see beauty.

ADDICTED

I am a junkie
For the pen
I need my fix
Of ink
Addictive
I can't stop
Gravitated grammatical warfare
I don't even fight it anymore
Keep going back to get
Another score
I'm Poeticc Serenityy
Yes,
I am a feen for
Poetry.

P.O.E.T.R.Y

P romise me, you will never leave me. I'm incomplete without you.

O nce you entered into my life, I realized you are kindred soulmate.

E lectric gratification with every stroke of the pen, there was a release.

T ransformation took place, I felt the urge to fly.

R eleased from my cocoon, emerged this butterflyy. Free, just you and me, Poetry.

Y our presence became part of me, you created Poeticc Serenityy.

HANDPICKED

Of all flowers in the garden
You handpicked me
I always thought of myself
As the weed
Unwanted
Misplaced
Known as the nuance
No beauty in me
What was my purpose
You began to water
My roots
You said you want to see me blossom
Flourish
Elude sweet fragrances
Expose my petals
They are now for
You to only see
My floral nectar is sweet
Edible garden,
Sample me.

DESIRE

You speak to me
Whisper,
Soft,
Promising sounds,
Linger from your lips.
Saying you saw me,
Looking for you.
You said, you were
Missing from my heart.
Flames died down.
You said, I had let you go.
I asked who you were,
You said,
Your Desire.

EYES WIDE OPEN

There, I said it,
With my eyes.
I know you heard them,
Speaking for me,
Because my lips are
Speechless.
Intense stares of longing.
You know I want you,
Shy no more,
Eyes Wide Open.

IF

If I was your butterfly,
Would you capture me?
Or
Set me free?
Would you paint my wings?
Or
Let them be?
If I was your flower,
In your garden,
Would you pick me,
To place me is a glass?
Display just for show?
Or
Leave me in fertile grounds,
Where I can continue to grow?
If I was a star,
Would you try to reach for me,
To hold tight?
Or
Leave me in the sky,
To continue to shine bright?
My Love,
What would you do with me?

LUST

Lust

Deception of love

Desire of the eye

Cousin of

Lies

Deceitful

Your flattery is a mirage

Setting the trap for the host

Beyond the body

You attempt to captivate the mind

But resisting temptation you

You must flee...

ALIVE

Midnight Madness,
Entangles my thoughts
Emptiness from your presence.
I feel abandoned.
Bed of grave,
Body cold
Clench the sheets of
Where your body once laid.
Warm mirage,
Ghost of your love
Remains besides me
Séance,
Calling out your name.
Return to me,
Possess this body
This is yours.
I've come back
Alive.

VAMPIRE KISS

My love,
Oh how I miss
Your
Vampire kiss,
No interview needed
I surrender my love to you
Blood of Hypnotic tonic
Running through my veins
Succulents bites of only pleasure
No pain
Forever we live in this
Eternal lovers bliss
Elevating
Floating over the stars
Sunlight doesn't burn us
Our passion does
Transform this night
Into day
Forever in your arms
I will stay
I'm marked with your aggression
I
Am
Yours.

JUKEBOX

I'm your jukebox baby
I'm your favorite tune
You can play me
Day and night
From the sun to the moon
Do you want classical?
Or maybe jazz?
You like country,
Or maybe bluegrass?
You might want some hard rock,
Or just rock and roll.
You seem the type that likes
Hip Hop and Soul.
Let me know your favorite genre
And that's what I will be.

NATURE'S SYMPHONY

This morning
I heard a little bird
Telling me a spoken word
Asking me did I hear her song
That she sings all day long.
Singing this tune,
I sing because I'm free
I want you to be like me
Sing with the glory in your heart
Not letting the cares of life
Tear you apart
Sing with me
This beautiful harmony
Nature's Symphony
Let them hear your song
I too began to sing
The song
That she sings
All day long.

FANTASY

I rather leave you,
In my fantasy.
In reality,
You might leave me.
In my fantasy,
You will forever
Stay
Closing my eyes.
I see you
Clearly
You and me.
Reality hits.
Poof,
You're gone.
Heartbreaks.
Going back to sleep.

ENCORE

She wakes up,
Singing with the birds.
Morning song, choir of nature
Harmonious, new dawning
Sun lights the stage
of the new day.
Standing ovation.
As the flowers bloom,
Encore.

HOLD MY DREAMS

I don't write to become
Famous.
I don't need my book to be a
Bestseller.
I want my book to
be made,
So my children can
hold my Dreams.

POETICC LOVE STORY PART ONE

Laying here,

Counting stars like sheep,

It's hard for me to fall asleep,

When you're not near.

You are my nocturnal peace.

Dream waves ride inside my mind,

I'm safe aboard your ship

Love boat,

Sailing away in the ocean abyss,

Horizon awaits our embrace

Yet, in my fantasy you are there

Reality, you're not here.

Pillow becomes my only comfort.

I cry out for you,

Only echoes,

Respond back.

Pictures only haunt my memories,

They only remind me of what used to be.

Once upon a time, it was you and me.

Now it's just

Me...

POETICC LOVE STORY PART TWO

My Queen,

I feel your tears, as you cry.

Because the sky began to rain.

I too, am awaiting for your love.

I miss your morning kiss.

You glowed in our bed, like the morning star.

Your warmth, from your smile,

Removed the cold shell from my heart.

Now we are apart,

I'm starting to feel chills again.

Arctic blast.

Please no more tears.

For it hurts that I'm the one that created them.

Soon, your king will return.

To kiss those soft petal lips.

My flower of the new day

Continue to bloom

I smell your sweet essence, here in my room.

Days become hours

Hours become minutes

Minutes become seconds

I'll be home to you.

CODE RED

Code Red ..Code Red
This is an emergency
Revive this love, in me.
Resuscitate this
Yearning, insatiable desires.
Dr. Love.
You have the cure,
It's not in a bottle,
But on your lips.
CPR
Caress
Press
Repeat.
Rapid heartbeat,
Beating like butterflies fluttering wings.
Can you hear them?
Through your stethoscope.
You are my antidote,
From this love ache.
No side effects.
I can take two of you now
And
One in the morning.
Discharged
This visit was well over due.

FIRST MEAL

You are refreshing as the first sip
Of orange juice in the morning
You awaken me like the aroma of bacon in the air.
You are the smooth butter in my grits.
You are the sweet savory syrup to my pancakes.
You are my first meal of the day.

VITAMIN C

Squeeze me
Like
Fresh juice
In the morning
Vitamin C
Papaya, mango with lemon
Sweet to the lips
Slow steady sips
Good morning.

12 O'CLOCK

I was running
The clock struck 12
I had to go, before I could
Give it you,
My heart.
It fell on the steps, as I was leaving.
As you go around town,
To try to claim its rightful owner,
Many tried to take hold,
But it only fits in one place.
You found me,
My King.
Come now,
Claim your Queen
Place it back,
It beats only
For you.

WELCOME HOME

My love,
Welcome home
Let me wrap
My arms around you.
Entangle me
Pull me in.
Make me into a
Knot,
So you can't
Untangle me.
Too long away you were.
Dawning of the sun
That changed into moonlight
Reminds me of the day
That I had to endure
Without you.
Oh, how I was saddened.
I appreciate your presence,
Evermore.
Now come in
And shut the door.

HISTORY

The blast,

From your past

Though it was only earlier today,

Seems like eternity

Longing

For the next embrace

This time

24 hrs ago

You were with me

I became you

You became me

Departure

This cruelty

Feels like the fallen of

Rome

Hurry, come back to me,

So we can once again,

Make history.

SPOON FED

Taste my words
Feeding you from my
Pen
Not exactly a silver spoon
Still just as precious
Leaving you desiring more
Maybe you are not greedy
And you are satisfied
Alphabet soup
Words in your mouth
Never gluttony
So may expressions
Inside me
Spilled like a glass of milk
Running over
Drink up
Does your mind good
You're welcome.

CHAPTER TWO

Tears of Pain

HEARTBREAK A-Z

Absurd Absurdity, was it for me to
Believe that you
Could only love me.
Delusional were my thoughts.
Every fiber of my being craved you.
Facetiously, you handled my heart.
Gambit pieces on your game of deceit.
Halfwit is what you called me.
Idiocy took over my mental stability.
Jeering at my tears, flowing free.
Karma will come like a boomerang.
Lacerations, your heart will feel.

Machinations you attempted, have failed.

Narcissism took over you like a plague.

Obfuscated your soul to be transformed.

Perpetrating fraudulent affections.

Quaffing down your lies, I choked

Realm of this nightmare, you created.

Sage protects me from your stains

Tangible emotions, I feel all the pain.

Unable to focus,

Vulnerable, open wide, you destroyed us.

Walking away, no need to look back.

X-rays cannot detect all of your damages.

Yearning for a touch of kindness,

Zaniness, is only what you left me.

I'M FINE

Lies

What a horrible being you are.

Stirring up

Mayhem

Strife

For your own pleasure

Demolishing, the path of your

Victims

You dress up in a white bow

To indicate that's it no big deal

But it's all the same attire.

Lie,

You are the blame

You present as only one,

Then you multiply.

You then become too much.

Those you ensnare,
Forget how many you are.
Hearts have been broken
Lives have been destroyed
All because of you.
You catch victims
In their weakness.
Tip of the tongue,
You lay
Waiting
Hoping
This would be the day
As a dragon of fire
You burn,
Another
Soul away.

ARE YOU LISTENING?

You want me to say words
That tickle your ear
Favorable words
You want to hear
What if I was a snake
Saying nothing
But a hiss
Do you still want this?
You probably do.
Oh, foolish one!
Despite my warning
You lean in further
You play with
Temptation

You're about to hear
Your Damnation
I'm about to give you
Your whisper
Last chance to walk away
I have you now
You are mine
Forever
In this inferno of fire
Yet, you still glow
Is this what you desired
Satisfied, another customer.

FOCUS

You caught me
Like a
Spur of the moment
Unaware of your
Advances
Secret glances
Hoping for
Circumstances
For you to
Make your
Move..
But you decided to,
Change your
Direction
From
My
Attention
Now
Feel
Stranded
Where did your
Focus
Go?....

FUNK OF DEPRESSION

Stand Back!!!

You are too close.

Always on my space

Invading

Complaining

No one wants you around

Walking cloud

You were gray

Hovering

Worst than the plague

Toil in agony

Mind games

Scrabble

You reek of

Death

Walking dead

No cologne

Can cover your stench

Almost had me

Funk of depression

Almost has me

*In **Your** feelings.*

VISITS

Sometimes, I want to cry
When I think of the times
Of no more
Nothing but nostalgia now
Memories seem more like
Ghostly visits
Faded
Afterthoughts
Floating around my
Cerebellum
Trying to stay
Relevant
I long for the
Now,
The tangible
Moments.
But all I have to
Hold on to
Is your invisible
Love..

SNEAK ATTACK

Sneaking up on me
I was not prepared
You never play fair
You usually attack
On the left
Or
On the right
Bringing me down
There is no fight.
You destroyed my day
My noon
My night.
Some think you are a
Figment of my imagination
I feel your sensations
Agony
Defeat
Once you have me down
I just want to sleep
Hoping you will go away.
You made yourself at home

You made it clear
This is where you stay,
You are happy here.
I promise,
You won't remain long
Pretty soon,
You will be gone
Annoying guest
Your visit is about to be
Over.
I'm about to take this
Your nemesis
OTC
2 every 4 hours
Finally I rid
Of you
Demon of eternal pain
Never welcomed
Go back,
to whence you came
cast you out
evil
Migraine.

TEARS OF A BUTTERFLY(Y)

Have you seen butterflies cry(y)

I do, when I see my sisters cry(y)

Tears fell unheard

They landed on flowers as morning dew

Because of the mourning that was due

From the heartache they(y) ensued

It's so faint

Because they(y) try(y) to hide the pain

They(y) should be flying free

But their wings are stuck

Help me, they(y) sing.

But no one can hear

Butterfly(y) Tears.

THE DOOR 2

I don't even get mad
Anymore
It's the same revolving door
At first I tried to change the lock
But you keep the key
This is exhausting me
Finding a treasure box
Within the dark sea,
Is easier than trying
To find out
If you truly love me.
I'm taking the door off the hinges
No more guessing
What's behind the door
Door 1
Door 2
Door 3
Whatever door you open
You won't find me.

CRIME SCENE

She asks, "What do you want me to do?"
"Are we together, or are we through?"
He was looking in her eyes
Distance grows
Love doesn't twinkle
Anymore.
When she spoke,
To say I love you,
He said, "Say anything but that."
She's taking back
No longer cupid's arrow
But the devil's dagger
Penetrates her heart
Eyes crying red
On white sheets she wept
Leaving evidence
Of the heart broken
Crime scene
Love Died.

REMNANTS OF LOVE

Remnants of love
Is what you left behind
Like a shadow dancer
Gliding to the echoes of melodies
That was once our favorite tune
Now
I tuned out
No longer covered under your
Shade
Only a mask
A masquerade
No longer a princess
Lost my glass slipper
Chasing after you
Time struck 12
I guess it's all over.

UPROOTED

I'm trying not to hate
But the things you do
Resonates
In my soul
Trying not to let bitterness
Take control
Need to uproot like a
Weed
Unearth this bad
Seed
I can't understand for the life of me
How can you be so heartless
Actions are thoughtless
Because
I'm thought of less

Oh, yes
I guess
It doesn't matter
You removed the ladder
You once used
To climb to my heart
Now, I'm laying here
Broken
Falling apart
You don't even turn around
Not even knowing
I'm on the ground
Crying the tears
Fertilizing soil
Roots tug at my soul
It's time to let go.

CHAPTER THREE

*Tears of **Strength***

YOUNG KING

The aura of you light

Is

Brighter than you will ever know

Illumination follows you,

Even in your

Darkness

Despite your pain

You flash a shot of you smile

Contagious

The energies of inspiration

Aspiration

Example of the generation
That upholds a higher standard
Mighty lion, full of courage
Your roar is your words
You use to encourage
Young king
Bright sun
This work in you
Has only
Just
Begun.

STRETCH MARKS AND SCARS

Stretch marks and scars
Follow the trail of my life's story
History is all over me
See this here
Above my naval
Shows the strength of my motherhood
Expansion of skin
Where my babies were
Within me
These marks on my thighs
Shows growth of my womanhood
Body changes form
Beautiful
My hand beholds a scar
From not being cautious
Slight burn from the oven
But worth the meal I was able to prepare
Skin reminds me of
My life's journeys
Road map of life
Travel with
Me.

UNDERSTAND

Baby,
I need you to understand
I gotta be the man
I need you to have my back
I'm under
Constant attack
Just for being black
I'm doing the best I can
Making ends meet
Food on the table
Shoes on our kid's feet
Scrutiny
Humility

It's what I endure
Every time I walk out that door
I pray I can turn the key
To walk in once more
My job is to provide, love and guide
My Queen
I need you by my side
I'm so blessed, my angel
Crown of a halo
I see all of you do
I simply adore you
Take my hand, we got this,
All the way to the Promise Land.

DADDY / BABY GIRL

Daddy

You are the bestest

Better than the restest

You are the greatest

My everything

Don't ever leave

I love you

Baby girl

You are my entire world

Forever I will hold your hand

I will protect, love and provide

Daddy's right here

Always by your side.

LOOK AT HER

Look at her
Innocent and lovely
Her thoughts should only be carefree
Look at her
I only want to see her beautiful smile
My cherished lotus flower
Look at her
The blessings of my soul
Her presence makes me whole
Look at her
Child with an angelic face
Heart of love and grace
Look at her
Image of me
But she owns her own
Identity.

VICTORY

Don't give room for the
Enemy to enter in
Have to fight
Can't let it win
Comes like a sly fox
Or
A lovely gift box
Beware of the sender
This is not a lender
It wants to stay
To take away your joy
That's always the ploy
But let me encourage you
Despite what the enemy may try to do
It can't defeat
The solider in you
So continue to stand
Put on your shield
Guard your heart
Let's go prayer warriors
Time for that devil to flee
Right now
Claim your
Victory.

PERIOD

You say I dance around your
Mind with my words
Nouns, adjectives, verbs
Collectively, turns into thoughts
I just want you to read me.
Excited, exclamation point.
Am I hard to understand, question mark.
Maybe, it's best if you just
Close my book, Period.

BUTTERMILK BISCUIT

You said I'm your buttermilk biscuit
But all you try to do is sop me up,
With your gravy of guilt
Whisked my thoughts
Mashed my mind
I'm no turkey
This meal
No left over's
Dinner is done
No desert for you
This sweet potato pie
You already cut your slice
Wipe your mouth
Clear the table
Your dinner is done.

W.R.I.T.E.

Get your pen
And begin to
Extract those feelings from within
Let your tears flow
Through the ink
Tell of your story
That only you
Can tell
It's time to
Come out of
Your shell
This page is left
Blank for you

Write on

Write on

Unmask

The writer in

You

Finally let

Your soul

Shine through

So again

I tell you,

Get your pen

And begin

To extract those feelings from within.

ROSE PETAL RED

She reaches down in her purse
To retrieve her mirror
Trying to check for imperfections
And errors
She felt her lipstick was missing
Grabbed her favorite shade
Rose Petal Red
Gliding smooth across her lips
Same color matched her finger tips
She glared in the mirror, one last time
To make sure everything was fine
But then a thought came to her mind
A voice sounded like it was coming from
Behind.
The voice said to the girl
With the red lips,
You don't need any of this
Take this tissue
Time to give the world
The real
You.

RISE

Yes
I will rise
Standing right before your
Very eyes
Don't look surprised
The illumination of my energy
Lights any room
Bright burning sun rays
Beams through
Don't' stare, I'm like a
Solar Eclipse
Their lips
Words flow like a deep abyss
You want to come close to this
You will drown in my oceans
Of Dreams.

Let me preserve your life
Still humble and reserved
You won't see every curve
Not all deserve to see
My formation that embodies me
Sweetness eludes from my pours
I am a walking honeysuckle
But can change to a Venus fly trap
I suggest you stand back
Admire from afar
Sorry,
You can't open this
Honey jar.

I AM FORMED

Your hands feel like
They are sculpting my body
Creating the form as if I
Was clay
Molding me with the image of
Your imagination
Seeking gratification
Fingers slowly sliding long
The curvature
Leaving fingerprints as your
Markings
From top to bottom
From bottom to top
Formation
Has began
With the loving touch
Of your
Hand.

TEMPTATION 2

Tip toe,
Tip toe,
Slip
Temptation
Tripped you
Has you fallen.
He's smiling down
He thinks he caught you.
But him, not knowing,
You are able to
Get up
And leave the trap.
He didn't catch you
By choice
You were able to
Escape
Temptation,
Going back to his
cage.

PLANTED

My roots stayed
Planted.
Even though
Your leaves
Left
In
The
Wind.

DON'T WAIT

Don't wait until I fully bloom
To notice me
I need those around me,
that continued to
Water me,
When I was only a seed.

BEST FRIEND

You take me places,
Where I can only imagine.
You say everything, I was thinking.
You allowed me to take
Hold of you
And
Have my way.
The way you feel in my hand,
Perfect grip
Thank you for being my
Best friend
Thank you my
Pen...

Thank you for catching my TEARS!

Made in the USA
Coppell, TX
05 August 2020

32440473R00044